To Monica,

Merry Christmas-
Be a good girl all
year long.

Love
Santa
Claus

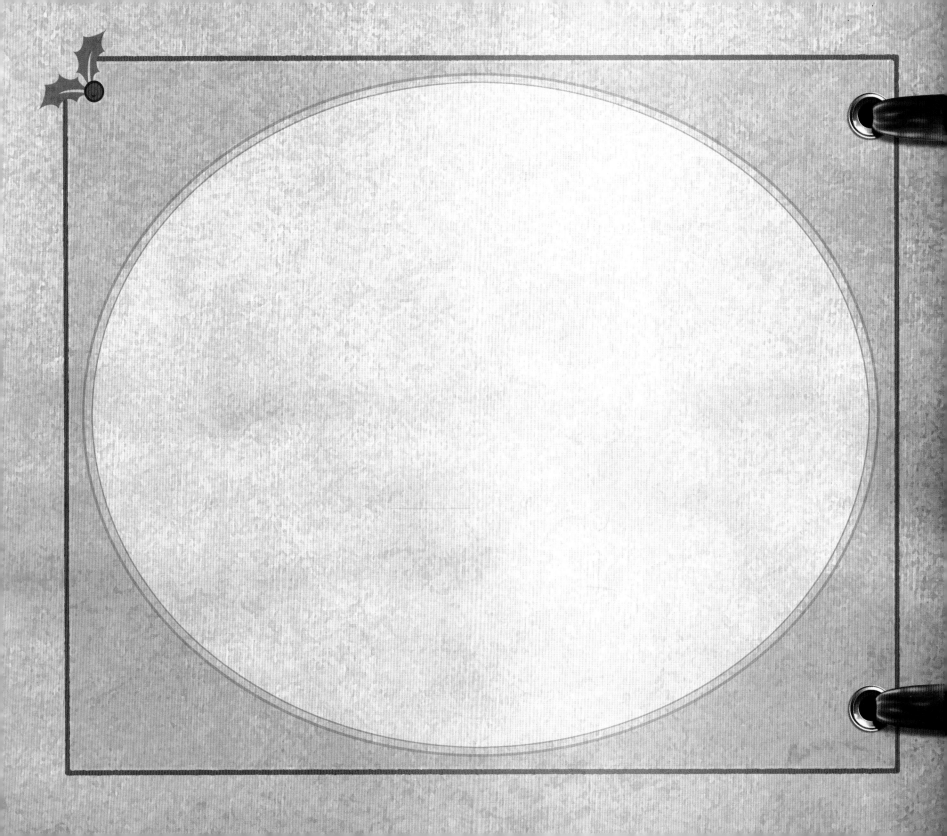

Santa and Me

written by
Erik Jon Slangerup
with **Joshua Janes**

illustrated by
Joshua Janes

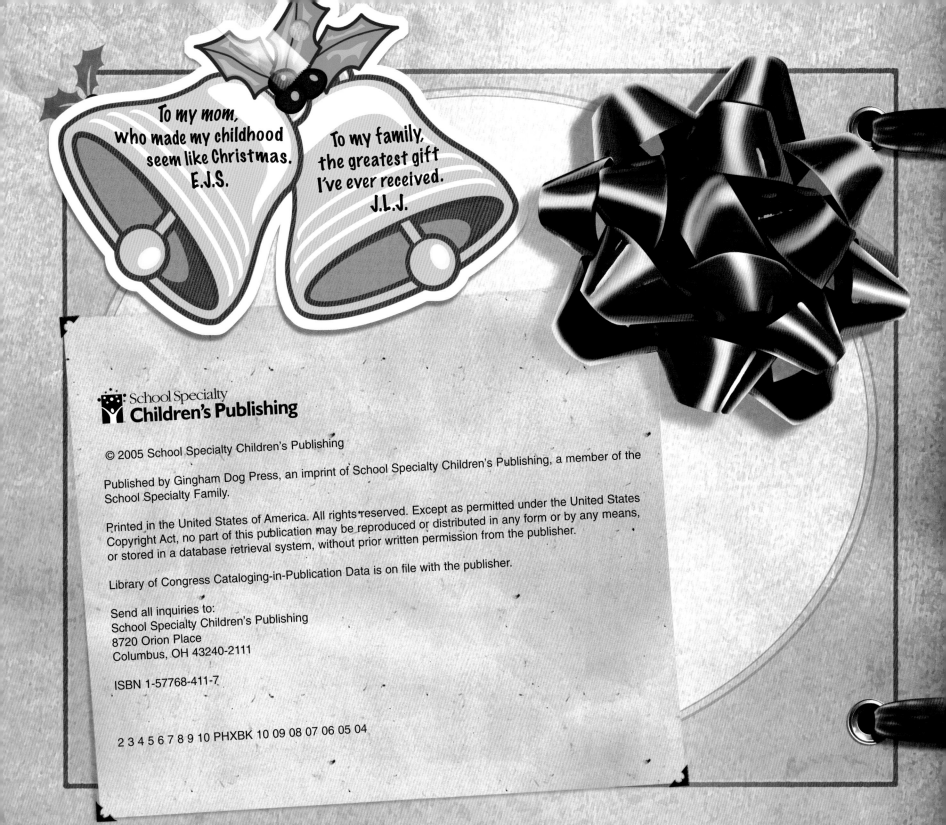

To my mom,
who made my childhood
seem like Christmas.
E.J.S.

To my family,
the greatest gift
I've ever received.
J.L.J.

School Specialty
Children's Publishing

© 2005 School Specialty Children's Publishing

Published by Gingham Dog Press, an imprint of School Specialty Children's Publishing, a member of the School Specialty Family.

Library of Congress Cataloging-in-Publication Data is on file with the publisher.

Send all inquiries to:
School Specialty Children's Publishing
8720 Orion Place
Columbus, OH 43240-2111

ISBN 1-57768-411-7

2 3 4 5 6 7 8 9 10 PHXBK 10 09 08 07 06 05 04

To: Santa

From: Mrs. Claus

Happy Holidays!

Dear Children,
I made this scrapbook so you could enjoy
some favorite memories of my life with
Santa. I have tucked in a few
secrets, too, but don't tell Santa.

–Mrs. Merrie H. Claus

The first time I met Santa, he had just won the Snow Festival Sleigh Race. I'm sure you can guess what he did with the prize money. Santa has always been a generous soul. That's what I liked most about him, next to the twinkle in his eyes.

SANTA

CHAMPION

Santa, what if we open a toy shop?

Merrie

Possible
Santa's

WINS!

Santa wins fifteenth consecutive sleigh race

By Broc Lee
N.P. North Star Reporter

...ream of miracles, but this man ...talking about

He won first place every year and used the prize money to buy toys for the neighborhood children. I suggested that he open a toy workshop. Then he could make toys to give to children all around the world. He thought that was a wonderful idea.

SANTA WORKSHOP

SANTA

PLEASE PUT TOOLS BACK

Photo by Joshua's...

Lots of people wonder why we moved way up here to the North Pole. Santa says that he loves the cold weather. I'll let you in on a little secret, though. Warm weather makes Santa a little sleepy. He'd never get all those toys delivered if we lived in Florida.

A CLIMATE OF SLEEP?

written by Tess Toob

For years, people have been moving to places like Florida, California, and the Bahamas to relax in the sun. Now, after a 10-year study done by Dartnose University, they have scientific proof that warm environments make people sleepy.

When asked why the study took so long, **Dr. Ben Napping** was quoted as saying, "We would have completed this research nine years ago, but we fell asleep."

During this study, professional lab rats **Billy Big Ear** and **Sirus Long Tail** were enlisted to participate in this

LAB RAT A

Name: Sirus
Age: 3
Climate: Tropical
Temperture: 98˚
Status: Napping

LAB RAT B

Name: Billy
Age: 3
Climate: Polar
Temperature: -2˚
Status: Alert

Santa's Christmas toy business grew bigger than our wildest dreams! We get toy requests from Picketsville to Paris and everywhere in-between. Santa had to train dozens of elves to help him make the toys. We had to add a second floor to our workshop—and a third—and a fourth. Last year, we even opened an office in Iceland.

SANTA'S WORKSHOP
281 ICE CASTLE AVE, NORTH POLE, NP 12934

NAME: Wanda Phull
EMPLOYEE #: 3789202897732-2

Wanda Phull

LEVEL 2 SECURITY CLEARANCE

DONNER

At first, getting Santa to fly wasn't easy. He preferred to travel on the ground with his sled dogs.

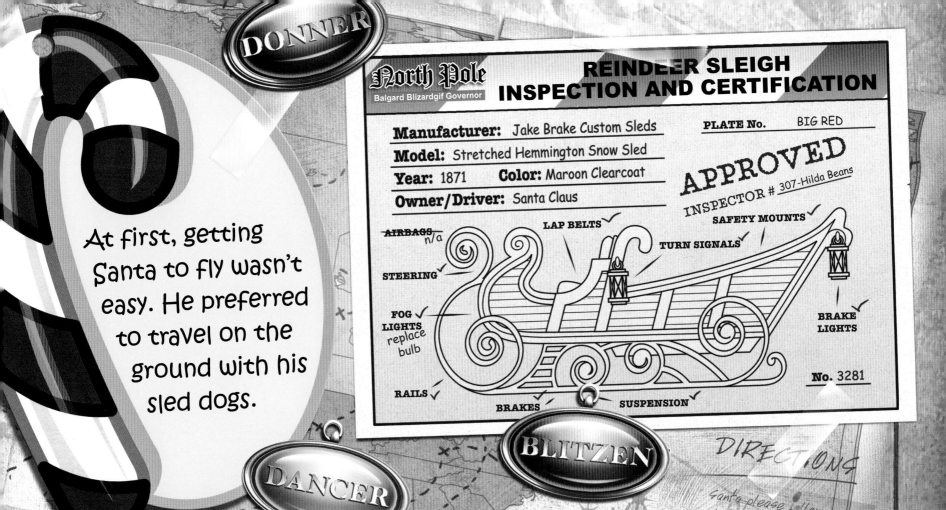

North Pole
Balgard Blizardgif Governor

REINDEER SLEIGH INSPECTION AND CERTIFICATION

Manufacturer: Jake Brake Custom Sleds

Model: Stretched Hemmington Snow Sled

Year: 1871 **Color:** Maroon Clearcoat

Owner/Driver: Santa Claus

PLATE No. BIG RED

APPROVED

INSPECTOR # 307-Hilda Beans

AIRBAGS n/a
LAP BELTS ✓
TURN SIGNALS ✓
SAFETY MOUNTS ✓
STEERING ✓
FOG LIGHTS replace bulb ✓
BRAKE LIGHTS ✓
RAILS ✓
BRAKES ✓
SUSPENSION ✓

No. 3281

DANCER

BLITZEN

DIRECTIONS

Santa please follow directions very carefully. We have put together new route

PRANCER

FLYING NOT JUST FOR THE BIRDS!

by Missy Taek

For as long as folks can remember, there have been wide-open skies. This vast blue wilderness has been the playground to every winged beast on the planet. But after several years of study, the scientists at the Aeronautic Institute for Research (AIR) have made a startling discovery. A small, select species of reindeer found only at the North Pole can actually fly! When Mrs. Claus and the elves heard this amazing news, they immediately contacted AIR for more information. Flying reindeer might be the

The elves made Santa this wonderful map for his Christmas deliveries. Unfortunately, he wasn't able to use it. We just refer to it as the "Great Hot Chocolate Mishap."

The first time Santa flew with the reindeer, people thought he was saying, "Ho-Ho-Ho!"

They didn't realize that Santa had lost control of the reins. He was actually shouting, "Whoa! Whoa! Whoa!"

SANTA'S FIRST FLIGHT

If he had feathers you

was a bird

By

.P. No

t wa

Always remember
your seatbelt.

Look both ways
before crossing
the sky.

Wear clean und

Check weather
forecast before

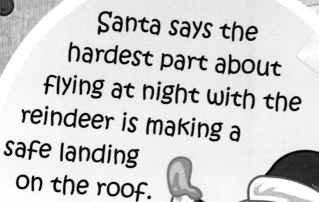

Santa says the hardest part about flying at night with the reindeer is making a safe landing on the roof.

ms new ... ... g ... e way
e world travels and ... es. This high-
... h engine runs completely on candy
... s and gum-drops. Making it very

so many people want ... ...
although it may completely de ... roy ...
oil industry, inventor Phillip Nott ...
thinks the world will be a lot sw ... te ...

...STUCK!

morn ... ...
that night. Really ... ...
not a creature was stirring. ... ...
even hear a mouse.

At 12:31 AM, there arose quite a noisy clatter on my roof. I jumped from my bed and ran to the window to see what might have happened. A large group of my neighbors was standing in my front yard, peering up at my roof. When I ran outside to join them, I discovered a red-suited person stuck upside-down in my chimney with legs kicking and flailing around.

Six tiny reindeer sat dazed and confused in the bushes alongside my house. Obviously, Santa had either misjudged the landing or forgotten to put on the parking brake. What a mishap! I called the fire department and the police. They greased the chimney with care in order to slide

Photo by Belle E. Botton at the Smith family home.

Santa now is going to take classes on th ...

ROBBIE BENKS

Stealth Training!

Are you loud and clumsy?
Do people hear you coming from a mile away?

Then you need stealth training from an experienced professional. In just a few hours, Robbie Benks can teach you how to improve your balance and move quickly and quietly. No more worries about tripping in the dark or getting stuck in chimneys.

Robbie uses the latest stealth technology to help you become invisible to the people around you. By signing up for classes now, you will receive the newest model of the Squint-Eye Starlight Night Vision 10x goggles as part of your enrollment fee.

> *"I used to be extremely clumsy. I had no stealth capability at all. After a three-month sentence with Robbie, I can now sneak past anybody!"*
>
> **Jimmy "The Knuckles" DeLuca**

'CALL NOW!
5

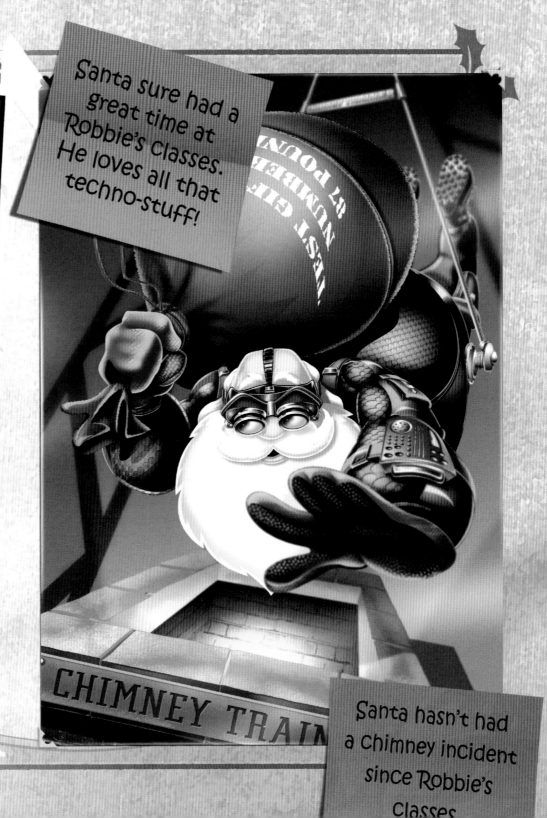

Santa sure had a great time at Robbie's classes. He loves all that techno-stuff!

CHIMNEY TRAIN

Robbie has really turned things around. He had been on the Naughty List for eight years, but has stayed on the Nice List ...st three years.

Santa hasn't had a chimney incident since Robbie's classes.

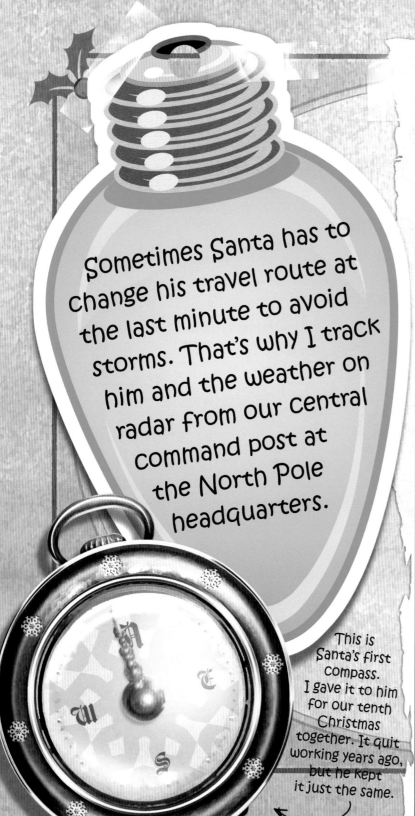

Sometimes Santa has to change his travel route at the last minute to avoid storms. That's why I track him and the weather on radar from our central command post at the North Pole headquarters.

This is Santa's first compass. I gave it to him for our tenth Christmas together. It quit working years ago, but he kept it just the same.

SANTA CHASERS

PRESIDENT: DUSTY ROAD

THE HOLIDAY SEASON WILL BE HERE IN JUST A FEW SHORT MONTHS, SO SIGN UP NOW TO JOIN THE SANTA CHASERS. IF YOU WANT TO BE AMONG THE FIRST TO SIGHT SANTA MAKING HIS CHRISTMAS EVE DELIVERIES, CONTACT DUSTY ROAD, PRESIDENT OF SANTA CHASERS.

JOIN THE S.C. NOW!

DUSTY ROAD IS A RENOWNED SANTA CLAUS PHOTOGRAPHER. HE WAS THE FIRST SANTA-CHASING JOURNALIST TO PURSUE SANTA AS A FULL-TIME, YEAR-ROUND CAREER. DUSTY FEELS THAT IT IS HIS DUTY TO BRING PHOTOS OF SANTA TO EVERYONE.

HAVE YOU SEEN HIM? SANTA S.C. SAN-RAD

One foggy Christmas Eve, the reindeer couldn't see each other or Santa at all. They stumbled on their landings and backed into Santa on the rooftops a few times. Since then, I always attach jingle bells to their harnesses, the sleigh, and Santa's cap. That way, they can hear one another even if they can't see each other.

CHRISTMAS

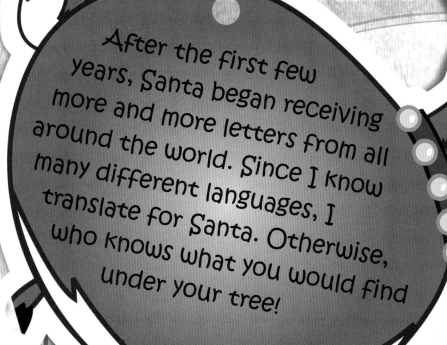

After the first few years, Santa began receiving more and more letters from all around the world. Since I know many different languages, I translate for Santa. Otherwise, who knows what you would find under your tree!

Santa flying over Paris, France.

The Secretary of the North Pole ...ests all whom it may concern to permit the citizen/ ...onal of the North Pole named herein to pass ...ut delay or hindrance and in case of need to ...give all lawful aid and protection.

SIGNATURE OF BEARER
NOT VALID UNTIL SIGNED

092

North Pole PASSPORT

Dantelti Hizzildafizzil President

Type
E

Surname
WITME

Given Name
CHER

Nationality
NORTHPOLEAN

Date of Birth
5/10/1902

Sex
F

PASSPORT NO.
247206534892

HT 3-7   WT 87   Hair BLN
Eyes BLK   Type ELF

OFFICIAL SEAL OF THE NORTH POLE   No. 14

Place of birth
ANTARCTICA, OUTPOST 372

E-NORTHPOLE--CHER--------------------------------
247206534892----------------ELF-W3E-D42B------------------67
--------CLASS-E----TRAVEL--323455----------QI

Cupid at
The Great Wall of China.

I traveled to
Egypt and all I got
is this crummy
shirt!

Santa at the four
pyramids in Egypt.

JOSE DELBO

OCHO DE LA TIENDA

MEXICO CITY

Diana Richardson

Horse Carriage Centre

Queen's Bridge

Privy, London LM4 1TP

UK

SANTA
281 ICE CASTLE AVENUE
NORTH POLE, NP 12934

These are
just a few of
Santa's favorite
Christmas
letters

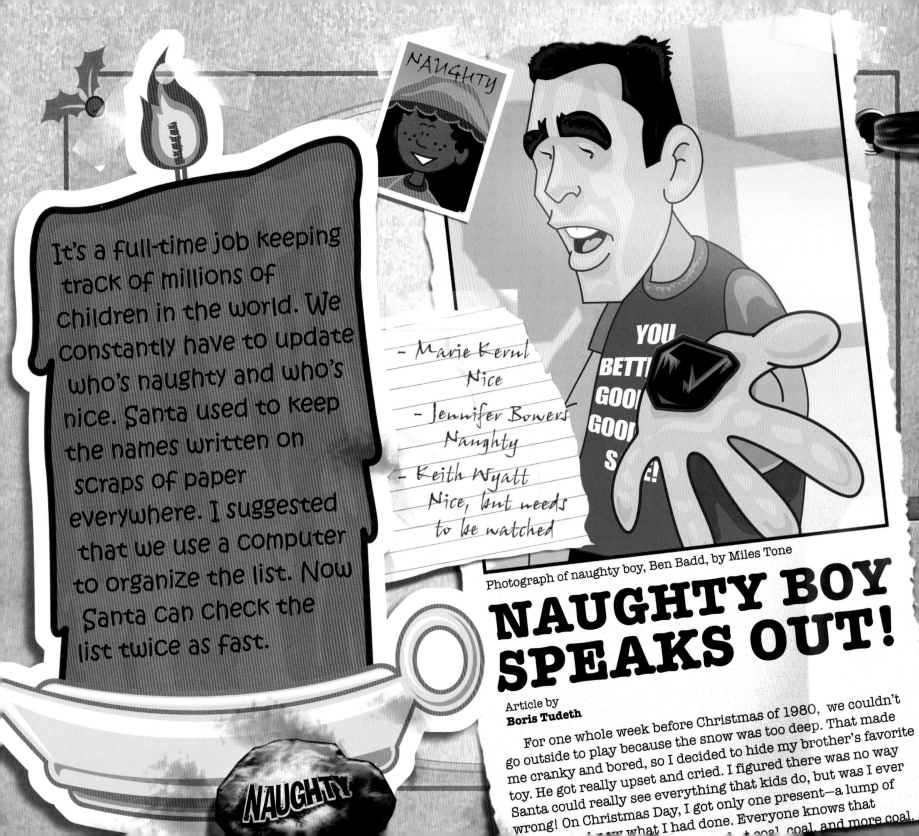

It's a full-time job keeping track of millions of children in the world. We constantly have to update who's naughty and who's nice. Santa used to keep the names written on scraps of paper everywhere. I suggested that we use a computer to organize the list. Now Santa can check the list twice as fast.

NAUGHTY

- Marie Kern?
  Nice

- Jennifer Bowers
  Naughty

- Keith Wyatt
  Nice, but needs
  to be watched

YOU
BETTI
GOOI
GOOI
S

Photograph of naughty boy, Ben Badd, by Miles Tone

NAUGHTY BOY SPEAKS OUT!

Article by
Boris Tudeth

For one whole week before Christmas of 1980, we couldn't go outside to play because the snow was too deep. That made me cranky and bored, so I decided to hide my brother's favorite toy. He got really upset and cried. I figured there was no way Santa could really see everything that kids do, but was I ever wrong! On Christmas Day, I got only one present—a lump of coal, coal, and more coal.

Santa loves to sing Christmas Carols, but he couldn't carry a tune if Christmas depended on it! After years of putting up with his singing, the folks at the North Pole planned a huge group sing-along.

We gave Santa this pitch pipe to help him stay in tune, but he said he had a natural singing voice and didn't need it.

SANTA, STILL SINGING?

Could your hearing possibly be at risk?

By Ginger Bredd
N.P. North Star Reporter

For years, Santa has spread joy and happiness with his toys, gifts, and good tidings. Unfortunately, his singing has not. No one can question San... s with all his heart and ... spirit. He just doesn't sin... sense of rhythm or the beat. Mrs. Merrie Claus has ...ately to get Santa to take

...MAS?

To: Mrs. Claus
From: Trey Bien

They figured that, if they sang loud enough, they could drown him out. It turned out to be great fun. Since then, people have been caroling in groups every Christmas. As always, Santa still joins in!

Santa needs to make sure he delivers the right gifts to the right children. I help him get organized. Each year, he chooses different colors of wrapping paper for different parts of the world. He also knows which children get presents without wrapping paper.

GLUE SNAFU

article by Ben Stukk

This Christmas created a sticky situation. Actually, it was more of a NON-sticky situation. The gift tag glue was incorrectly mixed, causing all of the gift tags to fall off their presents. The entire elf staff worked overtime to sort out the problem in time for Christmas Eve delivery. To avoid problems next year, Santa has decided to purchase a new packaging machine. This machine, named

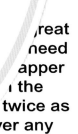

...e ...reat ...need ...apper ...the twice as ...ever any best value of ...s great energy ca... running for 20,000 hours straight without maintenance.

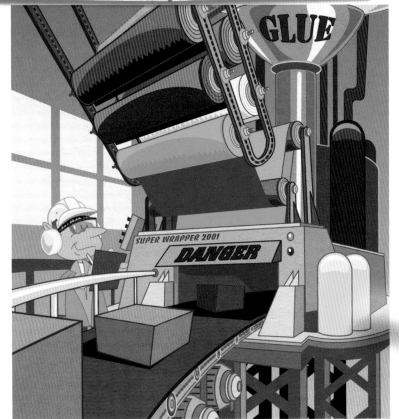

WRAPPING PAPER FIASCO!

MACHINE BREAKS DOWN, ELVES EXHAUSTED!

The Super Wrapper turned out not to be so super.

EMERGENCY ELF CREWS CALLED

FIRST SHIFT
- Gene Yus
- Pete Za
- Tom Atoe
- Chip Dip
- Candy Mann
- Lucey Lipps
- Bea Nyce
- Barbie Que
- Flo Rida
- Hugh Stun
- De Sill
- Ray Sin
- Dee Tour
- Ty Tann
- Sal Vage
- Sam Witch
- Gail Winds

SECOND SHIFT
- Al Armm
- Ron Away
- Dora Bell
- June Bugg
- Cal Sium
- Stew Deo
- Joy Pholl
- Ben Efit

Santa loves cookies. Since children leave plates of cookies for him every year, he is now considered an expert. He even judges cookie-baking contests. He still thinks my chocolate chip cookies are the best in the world, though.

Santa cookie review

article by Santa Claus

REVIEWING:
Mrs. Jia Ning's Super Secret Sugar Cooki

RATING: ★★★★

Mrs. Ning's Super Secret Sugar Cookies are definitely SUPER! They are a delightfully light and sweet Christmas treat. I tried to get the recipe from Jia, but

MAJOR UPSET IN COOKIE-EATING CHAMPIONSHIP

article by Ginger Bredd

It was an astounding upset at this year's annual cookie-eating competition. Four-year reigning champion Santa Claus—affectionately known as "The Big Red Cookie-Eating Machine"—was unseated by nine-year-old newcomer Kevin "The Cookie-Cravin' Kid" Myers.

This third-grader from Overland Park, Kansas, ate up the competition and left us wondering where a boy of his small stature could put all those cookies. Cookie-Cravin' Kevin consumed a record-breaking 201 sugar cookies in just five minutes! This beat the previous eating record of 197 sugar cookies set by Shane "The Giant" Hill from Alberta, Canada.

Shortly after Cookie-Cravin' Kevin wiped the last cookie crumbs from his mouth, an agent from the USA Professional Eating Team quickly signed him to a contract. Sadly, this mighty little eater will not compete in next year's championship.

Cookie
CONNOISSEUR

DEC 2003

US $2.95

Canada $4.95

Can cookies and milk
help you sleep?

What Is the World's
Favorite Cookie?

BRING OUT THE
BAKER IN YOU!

COOKIE EATING
1
CHAMP

SAN A'S CHOICE

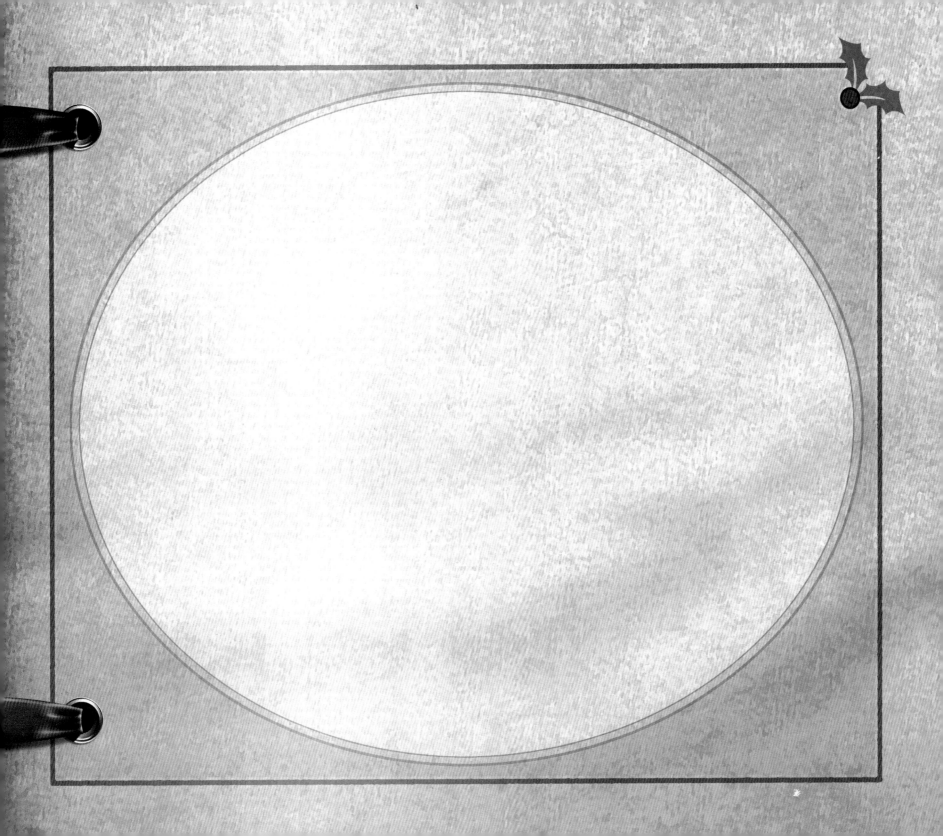

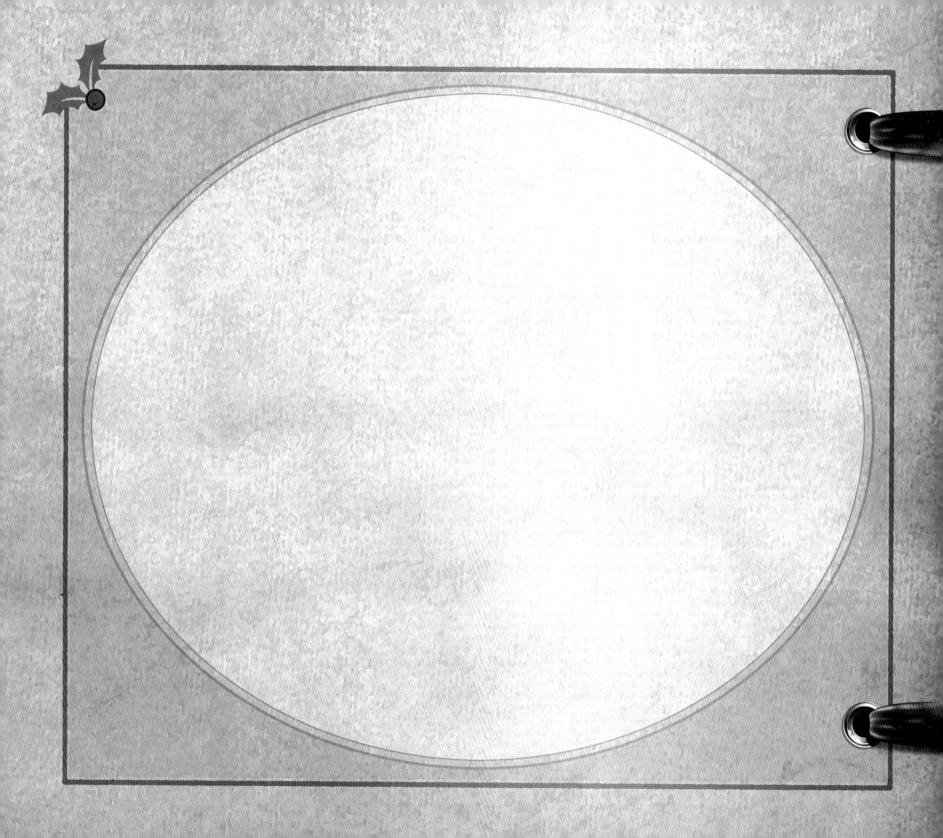